TO: . . . .
A magical story
for a magical you

From:

One sunny summer's morning Kendall was playing in her garden.

Suddenly she heard sniffling and crying coming from behind a leafy tree.

4

Kendall
tiptoed closer and closer
to the whimpering.

When she peeked around the tree
Kendall was shocked to see a
little white and purple, sad-looking...

5

UNiCORN!

"Hello, my name is Kendall,
what's your name and why are you
crying?" she asked the unicorn.

"I'm Sparkle, and I've lost all the magic colours on my rainbow horn from giving out **too many wishes**," said the unicorn.

"That's terrrrrible!" exclaimed .....Kendall.... "HOW can I help you get your magic back?"

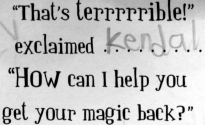

8

"Well," said Sparkle, "as I become happier colour returns to my horn and when I have all seven COLOURS my magic powers are restored and I can give out wishes again."

9

Kendall had a think, and a wonder and a ponder...

...what could she do?

"I've got it!" shrieked Kendall

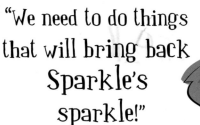

"We need to do things that will bring back Sparkle's sparkle!"

#1

SO, they tried playing a game of hide-and-seek.

Sparkle wasn't very good at it but because she enjoyed the game so much the first rainbow colour returned to her horn - ruby **RED**!

ching!

11

2

Then they sat on squishy bean bags drinking hot chocolate and eating rainbow-coloured marshmallows. This made **Sparkle** very happy!

slurrrp

With a slurrrp of her hot chocolate, brilliant ORANGE flashed up on her horn.

"I know what you need now," said Kendall . . .

"...a PAMPER day!"

So they wrapped up in fluffy robes, had their nails painted, and were so thoroughly **pampered** that sunny

#3

YELLOW

pinged back on to Sparkle's horn.

13

#4

Next up on their fun-filled mission was bouncing UP and down doing somersaults on Owen & Ker-lah's trampoline.

They were having so much fun that Sparkle's emerald GREEN band reappeared on her horn.

#5 Hungry from so much bouncing, the two friends went inside to make unicorn shaped cupcakes.

There was flour and eggs everywhere when the colour sky BLUE appeared on Sparkle's horn.

There were only two more colours to go and Sparkle was feeling SO much happier, but what could they do to get the last two?

15

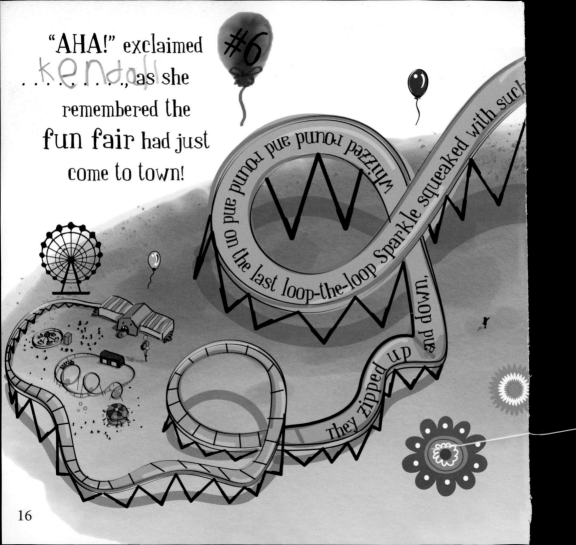

"AHA!" exclaimed ....kendall...., as she remembered the **fun fair** had just come to town!

#6

whizzed round and round and on the last loop-the-loop Sparkle squeaked with such

They zipped up and down,

...a bright INDIGO band appeared!

...elight...

There was just **one** more colour to go.

17

#7

Exhausted from all the fun
the two friends settled down to a
magical film and some **popcorn**.
Sparkle was **so** happy that
bold **VIOLET**, the very **last**
rainbow **colour**, popped
back on to her horn.

18

"That's it!
Thank you
. . . .!"
laughed Sparkle.
"You have made me
so happy that **all**
of my magical rainbow
COLOURS have
reappeared and I can
grant wishes again."

"Now, what wish
would YOU like?"
asked Sparkle.
"I wish, wish, wish
I could see the
Unicorn Kingdom,"
. . . . said hopefully.

19

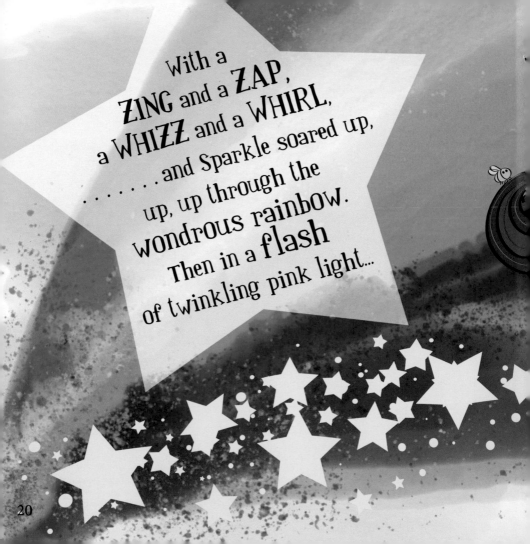

With a
ZING and a ZAP,
a WHIZZ and a WHIRL,
.......and Sparkle soared up,
up, up through the
wondrous rainbow.
Then in a flash
of twinkling pink light...

20

. . . . couldn't **believe** her eyes,
she was **really** there and all because she
had helped a **unicorn** have **oodles** of **fun!**

The End

COLOUR
ME IN